The Boxcar Children Mysteries

THE BOXCAR CHILDREN
SURPRISE ISLAND
THE YELLOW HOUSE MYSTERY
MYSTERY RANCH
MIKE'S MYSTERY
BLUE BAY MYSTERY
THE WOODSHED MYSTERY
THE LIGHTHOUSE MYSTERY
MOUNTAIN TOP MYSTERY
SCHOOLHOUSE MYSTERY
CABOOSE MYSTERY
HOUSEBOAT MYSTERY
SNOWBOUND MYSTERY
TREE HOUSE MYSTERY
BICYCLE MYSTERY
MYSTERY IN THE SAND
MYSTERY BEHIND THE WALL
BUS STATION MYSTERY
BENNY UNCOVERS A MYSTERY
THE HAUNTED CABIN
  MYSTERY
THE DESERTED LIBRARY
  MYSTERY
THE ANIMAL SHELTER
  MYSTERY
THE OLD MOTEL MYSTERY
THE MYSTERY OF THE HIDDEN
  PAINTING
THE AMUSEMENT PARK
  MYSTERY
THE MYSTERY OF THE MIXED-
  UP ZOO

THE CAMP-OUT MYSTERY
THE MYSTERY GIRL
THE MYSTERY CRUISE
THE DISAPPEARING FRIEND
  MYSTERY
THE MYSTERY OF THE SINGING
  GHOST
MYSTERY IN THE SNOW
THE PIZZA MYSTERY
THE MYSTERY HORSE
THE MYSTERY AT THE DOG
  SHOW
THE CASTLE MYSTERY
THE MYSTERY OF THE LOST
  VILLAGE
THE MYSTERY ON THE ICE
THE MYSTERY OF THE
  PURPLE POOL
THE GHOST SHIP MYSTERY
THE MYSTERY IN
  WASHINGTON, DC
THE CANOE TRIP MYSTERY
THE MYSTERY OF THE HIDDEN
  BEACH
THE MYSTERY OF THE MISSING
  CAT
THE MYSTERY AT SNOWFLAKE
  INN
THE MYSTERY ON STAGE
THE DINOSAUR MYSTERY
THE MYSTERY OF THE STOLEN
  MUSIC

THE HOME RUN
MYSTERY

created by
GERTRUDE CHANDLER WARNER

Illustrated by Charles Tang

SCHOLASTIC INC.
New York Toronto London Auckland Sydney
New Delhi Mexico City Hong Kong

Activities by Bonnie Bader
Activity illustrations by Alfred Giuliani

ISBN 0-439-12957-5

12 11 10 9 8 7 6 5 4 3 2 1   0 1 2 3 4 5/0

Printed in the U.S.A.   40
First Scholastic printing, April 2000

Contents

CHAPTER 1

A Broken-Down Baseball Park

"I wonder why they call this place the Half Moon Inn," said six-year-old Benny Alden. "I don't see any moons. Only that picture of a boat."

Benny and his big brother, Henry, were unpacking in their room in the country hotel.

"That boat is a famous ship, the *Half Moon*," Henry replied. He was fourteen and knew a lot. "In the early 1600s, Henry Hudson and his crew sailed the *Half Moon* up that river outside."

"The Hudson River!" Benny said.

A knock sounded on their door. Their sisters, Jessie and Violet, came inside.

"Aren't you guys done yet?" teased Jessie Alden. At twelve, she was the most organized. "We've been unpacked for ages."

"We've only been here thirty minutes," Henry pointed out.

"No wonder I'm hungry!" exclaimed Benny. "We haven't eaten since — "

"Lunch," ten-year-old Violet said with a giggle. "Plus you asked Grandfather to stop at that roadside stand for strawberries."

As if on cue, James Alden stopped by the open door. "I see the girls won the unpacking contest," he said with a laugh. "I'm off to meet the town council. I'll be back for supper."

"Is it okay if we look around town?" Henry asked.

"Of course." Grandfather gave him and Jessie some extra pocket money. "In case you want a snack."

"I will," Benny piped up.

Jessie put the money in her shorts pocket. Benny would never change!

Just that morning, after eating breakfast in their house in Greenfield, Connecticut, they waved good-bye to Mrs. McGregor, the housekeeper, and Watch, their dog, then piled into the station wagon. Hours later, they reached Pikesville, New York, a small town on the Hudson River. James Alden had been invited by the town council for his expert business advice on improving life in Pikesville.

"What a great summer day," said Henry as they left the inn.

The weather *was* perfect. But sunshine did little to perk up the dreary streets of Pikesville. Row houses marched one after the other, many in need of painting. Boarded storefronts added to the gloom.

"It's not very pretty, is it?" said Violet.

In fact, the town looked sad and neglected.

Henry agreed. "It's like it's been forgotten."

"That's why Grandfather was asked to come here," said Jessie. "He's helped places like this come alive again."

Benny pointed to an old redbrick building in front of them. "What is that?"

"Let's find out." Violet led the way down the broken sidewalk. They crossed a vacant lot overgrown with weeds to the front of the long, four-story building.

Large double doors were framed by dozens of small windows. Wire screened the windows, but most of the panes were shattered.

"It's a factory," Henry figured out. "A very old factory of some kind."

Jessie tapped a piece of chipped brick from the sidewalk with her sneaker. "It was probably nice when it was first built."

Just then the children heard a roar from behind the factory. Kids were booing and cheering.

"What's going on?" asked Violet, but Jessie and the others were already heading toward the back of the building.

They stopped in amazement at what they saw.

The factory had been built in an L shape. Nestled in the angle of the L was a ballpark!

"Neat!" Henry exclaimed. "What a great place to put a ballpark!"

A high fence with faded posters peeling from its crooked boards backed up against the brick sides of the old factory. The third side of the ballpark was bordered by the street, the fourth by a weed-choked empty lot.

Shaggy grass grew high in the outfield all the way up to the sides of the old factory. The infield was hard-packed dirt. A roofed grandstand had been built near the home base, where the corner of the empty lot met the road. The rest of the seats were splintery bleachers. Outside the foul line, beyond third base in the outfield, a rickety one-story clubhouse stood.

Teams of boys and girls were playing. A few people sat in the grandstand.

"Let's watch," said Jessie.

They climbed into the bleachers and sat next to a man about Grandfather's age.

"Who's playing?" Benny asked the gentleman.

"The team in blue shirts is the Hudson

Half Moons," replied the man. "That's the home team. They're playing the Catskill Eagles in the red shirts. Both teams are in the playoffs for the championship."

"What's the score?" asked Henry.

"The Catskill Eagles are leading," said the man, shaking his head. "I don't know how they're doing it. Our team is much better." He pointed to a girl a little older than Violet sitting in the dugout. "That's my granddaughter. Her name is Emily."

Emily had long brown hair worn in a ponytail pulled through her baseball cap.

"We're the Aldens," said Jessie. "This is my sister, Violet, and my brothers, Benny and Henry. I'm Jessie."

"Carl Soper. Pleased to know you." Mr. Soper shook hands with them all.

Violet said, "We play ball, too, back home."

"And where might home be?" asked Carl Soper.

"Greenfield, Connecticut," answered Benny.

The older man's brows lifted. "That's far

away. Just passing through the Hudson Valley?"

"No, we're staying here," Henry replied. "Our grandfather is working with the town council to help restore Pikesville."

Carl Soper grunted. "Restore! That's all you read about in the *Pikesville Star*. If they hadn't closed the hat factory, the town wouldn't have died. Now the town council has all these newfangled ideas to make Pikesville into a tourist spot."

"Don't you think it will work?" Jessie asked.

Instead of answering, Carl leaned forward, intent on the play down below. "What's going on?"

Jessie saw Emily Soper take a bat from the batboy. Emily swung the bat a few times to get the feel of it. Suddenly a man jumped off a bench. He wore a whistle around his neck and a red shirt.

"That's Coach Jenkins," said Carl. "He's the Eagles' coach."

Coach Jenkins took the bat from Emily with an apologetic smile and gave her another. Emily swung this bat and nodded that it was okay. Even from the grandstand, Jessie could see Emily looked puzzled.

"That's weird," she remarked. "Why would the other team's coach change Emily's bat?"

"Who knows? But my granddaughter is the best batter on the team," Carl Soper said proudly. "If anyone will win this game for the Half Moons, it'll be my Emily."

The pitcher wound up the pitch.

"Their pitcher looks pretty good," commented Henry.

Carl nodded. "His name is Danny. He's Coach Jenkins's little brother."

Danny threw the ball.

Crack!

Emily's bat hit the ground and she raced to first base. Her ball was still in the air. Emily danced at first, then decided to go for second. It would be close. She would have to slide, Jessie decided.

As she dove for the bag, the second baseman put out his foot, preventing Emily from finishing the slide.

Instantly the umpire came between Emily Soper and the Eagles' second baseman.

"Interference!" the Half Moons were yelling. The play was called fair and Emily was called out. The dark look on Emily's face showed her anger and disappointment.

Then the coaches got into the debate. The two men argued hotly and the umpire called a time-out.

Emily Soper hopped into the stands. Her grandfather handed her a soda from the ice-filled cooler at his feet.

"Did you see that?" Emily said. "Did you see Jason Baker stick his foot out? It was interference and the umpire called me out instead!"

"Yes, we saw," said Carl Soper.

Jessie noticed that Emily was holding her right arm.

"Is your arm okay?" she asked.

Emily glanced at her arm. "I'm okay. Who're you guys?"

"I'm sorry," said Mr. Soper. "Emily, meet my new friends, Benny, Violet, Jessie, and Henry. They are staying here with their

grandfather, who is in town on business."

"Nice to meet you," said Emily. She stuck her right hand out to Benny first and winced when he shook it.

"How bad is that arm?" asked her grandfather.

"I'll be all right." Emily drank the rest of her soda and went back to her team.

"She's a stubborn one," Carl said with a smile. "Just like all us Sopers."

Soon Emily was up at bat again. The Eagles led 10–3. Emily needed to hit a home run and bring the players in from the bases.

But from the way she held her bat, it was clear her arm was bothering her. She hit the ball, a pop fly. The first baseman easily caught it and she was out.

The game was over. The Hudson Half Moons had lost.

"Nice going, Emily!" jeered one of her teammates. "You're just as bad as old Home Run Herman!"

Henry wondered what the kid meant. Emily walked slowly to the stands and sat down heavily beside her grandfather.

"I lost the game," she said glumly.

"You hurt your arm," said Violet. "It was brave of you to go on playing."

Emily smiled at Violet. "Thanks. I'm glad somebody besides Gramps is in my corner."

"Do you live with your grandfather?" asked Jessie. The pair seemed very close.

"Yes, we're family," Carl Soper answered. "Ever since Emily's parents died."

"I was only four," Emily said.

"We live with our grandfather, too," Benny put in. "Our parents died and we went to live in a boxcar."

Emily looked at him with interest. "A boxcar?"

"It was empty," Henry explained. "And in the woods. We stayed there until our grandfather found us and took us to live with him."

"We still have the boxcar," added Jessie. "It's in our backyard. Grandfather had it brought there."

"Neat," said Emily. Then she remembered the ball game. "Brandon — he's our pitcher — thinks the Eagles are cheating, and so do I."

"What makes you think that?" asked Violet.

"The Eagles have won nearly every game this season," said Emily. "They *never* win this many games."

"Maybe they have better players now," said Henry.

"No," Mr. Soper said firmly. "Something is going on."

"Did you see me pick up that bat before I slid into second?" said Emily. "Then Coach Jenkins came over and took it away from me. He gave me another bat."

"That was strange," Jessie agreed. "Has he ever swapped bats before?"

Emily shook her head. "I don't know why he did it."

"To rattle you?" suggested Henry.

"Maybe," Emily said. "If the Eagles are cheating, how will we ever catch them?"

The Aldens glanced at one another.

Then Benny grinned. "Guess what? This is your lucky day!"

CHAPTER 2

The Doubleheader Case

Emily stared at Benny. "Why is it my lucky day?"

"Because we solve mysteries!" he replied. "We've solved cases all over the place!"

"Really?" Emily's brown eyes were wide.

Jessie chuckled. "Benny's bragging just a little. Sometimes we figure out mysteries."

Emily bounced with excitement. "Great! Can you find out if the Eagles are cheating?"

"We can try," answered Henry. "We're going to be here till Saturday."

"The championship game is Friday," said

Emily. "And we play again tomorrow. But how are we going to catch them?"

Violet thought for a moment. "Jessie's a good player. Is there a way she can join the other team as a substitute? That way she can watch from the inside."

"Good idea," Henry said. "Emily, have any of the Eagles been sidelined?"

Emily nodded. "Brian Preston hurt his knee yesterday. Jessie could take his place if Coach Jenkins will agree to it."

"This might work," said Henry. "Violet, Benny, and I can work the case from the outside. We'll watch the Eagles and see what they're doing. And if Coach Jenkins goes for it, Jessie will be checking out the Eagles from the inside."

"I feel so much better!" Emily said. "Even though I made the team lose today, we could still win the championship."

Her grandfather grunted. "And then it's all over. The youth leagues will be broken up."

"Why?" asked Jessie.

"It's a long story," said Carl.

"We have time," said Henry. "We don't have to be back at the inn for a while."

Carl Soper fished sodas from the cooler, passed them around, and the Aldens settled down to hear his story.

"Back in the early 1900s, Pikesville was a big town," Carl began. "Not like what you see today. Everybody worked in the men's hat factory. Baseball was the big sport in those days. Every town had its own team. The hat factory formed a ball club and built this baseball park right on the factory lot."

"Did people play during recess?" asked Benny, making them all laugh.

"Well, the factory wasn't exactly like school, but we did have a lunch hour and we could hit a few if we wanted," Carl said. "But the ballpark was built for our minor league team, the Pikesville Grays."

Henry shook his head. "I've never heard of them."

"There's a reason for that," said Carl. "The Grays had a great batter nicknamed Home Run Herman because he hit so many balls into the fence. In those days if you hit the fence, it was an automatic home run. Herman could have made it to the major leagues. Except for one big game."

Violet sipped her soda. Carl was a good storyteller. She couldn't wait to hear the rest.

Carl went on. "At the end of the 1908 season, the Grays were in the playoffs. Everyone knew they would win the pennant because Herman had been hitting home runs all season. The next game would bring the Grays fame. And put Pikesville on the map as an important baseball town."

"Were you there that day?" asked Benny.

Once again everyone laughed.

When Carl finished wiping his eyes, he said, "Benny, I wish I had been there that day. But I wasn't even born yet!"

Jessie nudged her little brother. "Emily's grandfather is about the same age as our grandfather. Grandfather wasn't around in 1908, either."

Carl continued the story. "But everyone in town was at the game, you can bet on that. These stands were packed. A lot of people bought expensive tickets to sit here in the grandstand. Some bought cheaper tickets to sit on those bleachers. The factory bigwigs had a special box down front. Nobody wanted to miss a single inning."

Henry could almost hear the sound of vendors calling, "Peanuts! Programs!"

Carl lowered his voice. "Yet it was the worst game Home Run Herman ever played. He didn't hit any home runs. He struck out again and again. The Grays lost the game and the championship."

"That's too bad," said Violet with a sigh. She had hoped this story would have a happy ending.

Carl nodded. "When the game was over, Herman's teammates were angry with him. They felt he had let them down. In the clubhouse over there, where the players had lockers to change from their street clothes into their uniforms, somebody found a twenty-dollar bill in the pocket of Herman's pants. Back then, twenty dollars was a lot of money. More than Herman made in a month at the hat factory."

"Where did he get it?" Jessie asked.

"His teammates figured Herman took a bribe to throw the game."

Violet was puzzled. "You mean, lose the game on purpose for money? Why would anybody do that?"

Carl shook his head. "No honest player would. But not all players are honest."

Carl sighed and went on, "Herman said that on his way to the game he had helped a lady whose motorcar had gotten stuck in a ditch and she had given him the money for his trouble. He also said he hurt his shoulder pushing the car. But no one else in the whole town had seen this lady. Nobody believed Herman's story."

"They sure gave up on their hero quickly," Henry said.

"Even quicker when the newspapers got hold of the story," said Carl. "It became a huge scandal. The story was picked up by papers as far away as New York City. The papers called for the mystery lady to come forth, but she never did. Pikesville was in disgrace."

Benny wondered about the baseball player. "What happened to Home Run Herman?"

"He left town," replied Carl. "He didn't leave a note or tell anybody. He just up and left. Home Run Herman was never heard from again."

The Aldens were silent for a moment after hearing such an astonishing tale.

"Nothing was ever the same," Carl concluded. "People blamed everything on Home Run Herman after that. If only Herman hadn't thrown the game, they'd say. Pikesville would be a big town still."

"Would it?" asked Violet. She couldn't believe that one man losing a single baseball game was the cause of a town falling into ruin.

"No," said Carl. "It didn't help that Pikesville was known for its cheating baseball team. But men's hats went out of fashion sometime after I began working in the factory. And then the factory closed. Some found other jobs in town, but many had to look elsewhere. It wasn't like the grand old days when everyone worked at the hat factory and the Pikesville Grays were the champions."

"That's a sad story," said Benny.

"You haven't heard the worst part," Emily told him. "Remember that name the kid called me when our team lost?"

"Yeah," said Jessie. "He said you were just as bad as Home Run Herman. What did he mean by that?"

Carl put his arm around Emily's shoulders. "Herman's last name was Soper. Home Run Herman was my uncle and Emily's great-granduncle."

"Everybody makes fun of our name," Emily said glumly.

"The funny part is that Emily is a great batter," said Carl. "Just like Herman was." He scratched his chin. "I'd give anything to have our name cleared. So Emily could play without kids comparing her to her great-granduncle."

Henry suddenly remembered something Mr. Soper had mentioned earlier. "You said the youth leagues are going to be broken up after the championship game on Friday. How come?" he asked.

Once more Carl grumbled. "Because the town council has pretty much decided to tear down this ballpark. The kids won't have anyplace to play in town. They claim in the *future* they'll build another ballpark out by the highway."

Jessie swallowed. Grandfather was here to help the town council fix up the town. But surely Grandfather wouldn't agree to tear down the ballpark? He always believed kids should have places of their own to play.

"They're going to turn the factory into one of those fancy mini-malls," Emily added.

"That won't be so bad," said Jessie. "At least the old factory won't be torn down."

"But why tear down the ballpark?" asked Benny. He thought the old grandstand and grassy outfield were neat.

"Because the council would rather have a big parking lot here." Carl Soper stood up, and everyone was quiet for a moment. "Well, Emily and I best be heading home," he finally said.

"You need to talk to Coach Jenkins about substituting on the Eagles team," Emily said to Jessie.

Henry stood up, too. "We'll be here tomorrow morning. I hope Jessie will talk Coach Jenkins into letting her play. We'll do everything we can to find out if the other team is cheating."

Emily smiled at them. "I'm glad you came to Pikesville. See you tomorrow!" She and her grandfather walked down the bleachers.

"Well!" declared Violet. "Looks like we have another mystery."

Henry held up two fingers. "Not just one mystery. Two."

"Two? What are they?" Benny asked.

Jessie knew. "First, we have to find out if the Catskill Eagles are cheating. And second, maybe we can find out what really happened to Home Run Herman."

"Two cases," said Benny, delighted.

"In baseball, that's known as a doubleheader," Jessie added, and she went down by herself to talk to Coach Jenkins.

CHAPTER 3

"The Factory Is Haunted!"

"Gosh, I forgot how hungry I was," said Benny as the waitress led them to their table.

"Well, that's a first!" Grandfather said, laughing. "What have you all been doing to make Benny forget his appetite?"

"It's really exciting! We can't wait to tell you," Violet said, unfolding her napkin in her lap.

"Let's order first," said Henry, studying the large menu. Like Benny, he was famished.

The Aldens had driven to the nearby town of Croton-on-Hudson to eat at a little seafood place on the river. Luckily, they were able to get a table by a window.

Benny was fascinated by a tugboat chugging up the Hudson. He would love to be the captain of his own boat someday.

"Benny, have you decided?" asked Jessie.

Benny picked up his menu. The choices were written in script. He could read, but only printing.

"They have a bacon burger," Jessie pointed out helpfully. "It comes with fries and a salad."

"I'll have that." Benny closed his menu, hoping there was something chocolate for dessert.

Jessie ordered the same. Violet and Henry chose tuna burgers and Grandfather decided on a salmon steak.

The waitress came back with glasses of water and bowls of tortilla chips and salsa. Grandfather ordered for everyone, adding a pitcher of lemonade.

"Now," said James Alden, "what have you been up to?"

"We visited a ballpark," Henry answered, dipping a chip into the spicy salsa. "It was behind an old factory."

Grandfather nodded. "I heard about that ballpark."

"Is it true it's going to be torn down?" asked Violet.

"I only sat in on one meeting today," said Grandfather. "But there was a lot of discussion about that ballpark. Do you know the history of it?"

Jessie sipped her lemonade. "A little. We watched some kids playing and met a man who told us about Home Run Herman and how he lost a game a long time ago."

"That's what I learned, too," Grandfather said. "Apparently this young ballplayer was caught with twenty dollars in his pocket. His teammates thought he had been bribed by the other team to lose."

"But nobody knows for sure what happened," Henry put in.

"Yes, but the scandal left its mark on this

town," said Grandfather. "That's one reason they'd like to tear down the ballpark. That way, they'll be rid of that old shame."

"But what about the kids who want to play baseball?" asked Benny. "Where will they go?"

"Mrs. Percy, who's on the council, said there are plans to build a new ballpark outside of town sometime in the future. No one could give me any more information. I only know this town wants to attract tourists and get young families to move here. Those are the things that keep a town alive."

Just then the waitress came with their meals. Plates were handed around and no one spoke for a few minutes except to ask for the ketchup or the salt.

"We're going to the playoff game tomorrow," Henry told Grandfather. "In fact, Jessie is substituting for a sidelined player."

"How did that come about?" Grandfather asked.

Henry told Grandfather of their suspicions about the Eagles, and that it had only taken Coach Jenkins five minutes of watching Jessie throw, catch, and bat before he agreed to let her play.

"Good," said Grandfather. "There's not much excitement in Pikesville. I'm glad you found something to do."

The kids looked at one another. They had two mysteries to solve. That was excitement enough!

Jessie was still confused over the fate of the ballpark. "Is the ballpark going to be torn down for sure?"

"The town council will vote Friday." Grandfather cut into his salmon. "The plan is to tear down the ballpark and make it into a parking lot for the mini-mall they will put in the old factory."

"A mini-mall?" queried Benny. He had been to malls before, but not a little tiny one.

"It's a large building that's been converted into small shops and restaurants," explained Grandfather. "The old hat factory is ideal. It's a solid building with plenty of space to divide into shops. And it's better than letting the building just fall down."

"That's good," said Benny.

Grandfather nodded in agreement. "There is one condition that might save the ballpark, but it's pretty slim."

"What is it?" asked Violet.

"The factory has already been declared historical and can't be torn down. If the property around it can be declared historical, too, then the town won't tear down the ballpark," said Grandfather. "But they need a very good reason to list the ballpark as historical. Right now the land is just a reminder of the old baseball scandal, and several members of the town council would like to see it paved over and made into a parking lot."

Violet looked at Henry. *So there is hope, isn't there?* her look seemed to say.

Grandfather asked, "Does anyone want dessert?"

"Does the sun rise in the east?" joked Henry.

"I don't know about the sun, but I want a chocolate sundae," Benny said, making them all laugh.

"I think you have a hollow leg," Grandfather said, ruffling Benny's hair. "Where do you put all that food?"

When dinner was over, they drove back to Pikesville. It was still light outdoors. Grandfather settled in the cozy sitting area with Bud Towers, the owner of the inn.

"May we take a walk?" Jessie asked Grandfather.

James Alden gave his permission. "Don't be gone long. You've all had a busy day."

Outside, the Aldens headed for the ballpark. Twilight was just beginning to close over the town.

"This is a good idea," Henry said to Jessie. "We have a chance to look for clues and talk about the mystery."

"Two mysteries," Benny corrected. "We have to find out if that other team is cheating — "

"And we need to find out what happened to Home Run Herman," Violet finished for him. "That's a pretty big job. We only have three days."

"We've solved tougher cases with less time," Henry said. "I don't think it'll be too hard to catch the Eagles at cheating — if they *are* cheating — with all four of us watching them."

"And I'll be on the team," Jessie reminded them. "I hope I don't make the other players suspicious!"

"You'll be fine," Violet reassured her older sister.

They reached the ballpark. Crossing the weed-choked lot, the children walked into the playing field. Shadows from the grandstand stretched nearly to the old clubhouse.

"It's a shame this place has to be torn down," said Jessie wistfully. "I wonder if we could do anything to help save it."

"Grandfather said if the council can find a good reason to make the ballpark historical property, it might be saved," said Henry.

"We've already got two mysteries to solve! Let's just add that to our list," Violet said lightly.

Then she looked beyond the ballpark.

The empty factory was shrouded in falling darkness.

She stared at the old brick building, letting her eyes adjust to the gathering gloom. Was that a light in that lower right-hand window? She rubbed her eyes. The light was gone. No, there it was, two windows away.

She grabbed Henry's arm. "Look," she said, and pointed to the pale yellow glow bobbing in the window.

"I thought that place was empty," Benny said.

"It is," said Violet. "Mr. Soper told us the hat factory closed years ago."

"I think we should go back to the inn," Henry decided. "We need to find out more about that place before we go hunting for clues."

Violet was glad. Usually she was ready to dive into a new case, but that light was spooky.

She shivered, though the evening was warm. The factory may have been shut down, but it was definitely not empty.

Someone — or something — was in there tonight!

The next morning, after a hearty breakfast of muffins, granola, juice, and scrambled eggs, the Aldens walked to the ballpark.

The teams were already on the field, warming up. Benny spotted Carl Soper in the grandstand and waved. He went with Henry and Violet to watch along the sidelines.

Jessie found Emily swinging a bat for practice out of sight of the Eagles. "How's your arm?" she asked her.

"It's okay," said Emily. "I want to thank you guys for helping me out."

"We haven't done anything yet," said Jessie.

"No, but you will." Emily was confident. "You told Coach Jenkins you can play center field?"

"Yes." Jessie nodded. "He made me show him my throwing and catching. Said I'm a fair batter, too."

"Good. I want you to meet our pitcher," Emily said as a dark-haired boy came up. "Jessie, this is Brandon. Brandon, this is Jessie Alden. She and her brothers and sister are going to help us."

Brandon nodded, looking around to make sure none of the Eagles players could hear or see them. "Emily said you guys solve mysteries."

"Sometimes," Jessie said modestly.

Then she heard Coach Jenkins whistle to get his team's attention and Jessie trotted out to join her team.

"You're ready to play?" he asked Jessie.

"Yes," replied Jessie. She knew center field meant a lot of running after fly balls.

Danny Jenkins, the pitcher, joined them.

"This is my brother Danny," said the coach. "Jessie is our new center fielder. I tried her out yesterday. She's pretty good."

Then Coach Jenkins gave Jessie a ball cap and matching red T-shirt to pull on over her regular shirt.

It was time to begin. The players took their positions.

It was hot out on the field, even though the game was starting early. Jessie adjusted the visor of her cap to keep the sun out of her eyes. The coaches argued again about the call at second base the previous day, which delayed the opening pitch. They really didn't seem to like each other.

Jessie glanced over at the factory. There were no lights in the broken windows this morning. Had they all imagined that light last night? Maybe it was some trick of dusk.

"Going to be a hot one today," commented Danny, who had left the pitcher's mound.

"I'm afraid so." She looked back at the factory.

"You keep staring at the hat factory," said Danny.

"Well, it's a very old building."

"It's more than that." Danny lowered his voice. "I see lights in there at night. The factory is haunted! I'd stay away if I were you!"

CHAPTER 4

A Message for Violet

Jessie tried to keep the shock out of her voice. "Are you sure? Maybe it's just the night watchman."

Danny shook his head. "Nobody guards the factory at night anymore. It's a ghost, I tell you!"

In the hot sun, Jessie felt a finger of ice trace her backbone. "Why would a ghost haunt an old hat factory?"

At that moment, the coaches stopped arguing.

"Got to go," Danny told Jessie. "I hear you're a great batter."

"Not great," said Jessie honestly. "Fair."

"We're all great batters on this team," Danny bragged. "Way better than the other team." He jogged across the diamond to the pitcher's mound and warmed up with a few practice pitches.

Then the umpire bawled, "Play ball!"

Danny threw the opening pitch. Emily was first in the batting order. Danny threw hard and fast to her. Emily's bat connected with the ball. Jessie watched as the ball sailed toward right field. The girl playing that position called the ball as she ran backward, glove held high. But she missed the catch and the ball dropped behind her.

By the time the girl picked it up and threw it to the infield, Emily was flying around the bases. She slid into third.

Jessie breathed a sigh of relief. The Half Moons were off to a good start.

In the grandstand in front of her, she could see Emily's grandfather. Benny sat beside him. Violet was watching from well behind home plate. And Henry was standing along the foul line. The plan was to change places every inning, so they could all watch from different viewpoints.

Benny saw Jessie in center field and waved. His sister was too far away to see him, though.

"Did you ever play baseball?" he asked Emily's grandfather.

"Did I ever! I love the game!" Carl Soper replied enthusiastically. "I played shortstop when I was in school and later working here at the factory. I coached our youth league years ago, and Emily loves baseball as much as I do. I guess we get it from old Home Run Herman."

"Emily is good," Benny remarked, watching her race to home base after the second Half Moons batter hit a single. The Half Moons were leading and had a runner on first.

"All the kids on our team are good," said Carl. "That's why we believe the Eagles must be cheating."

"How come?"

"Because they always lose the champi-onship to us," said Carl Soper, "except this year. Suddenly they're scoring run after run."

"The Eagles don't ever win?" asked Benny.

Carl shook his head. "Sometimes, but not like this. Wait till their team is up. You'll see. They'll be knocking the balls into the boards like crazy."

Benny stared at the peeling billboards way across the field. Right now a Half Moons batter was up. The boy smacked the ball high and out. While the kid skimmed the bases, bringing home the other player, the ball whacked into the fence. A home run.

Benny clapped, along with Emily's grandfather.

Meanwhile, Violet watched Danny as the ball sailed overhead. The big boy's face turned a dull red. He wasn't happy about the other team's first home run of the day. But Danny struck out the next player.

One fly ball caught and one Half Moons player struck out and the Eagles changed places with the Half Moons on the field. Jessie passed Emily.

"Good work," Jessie whispered to Emily as they passed each other slowly.

"Yeah," said Emily without looking at Jessie. "But you wait. The Eagles will hit every pitch out of the park."

Violet went to sit with Carl Soper, while Benny joined Henry on the foul line. He told Henry what Carl Soper had said about the Eagles hitting so many home runs during this season's championship.

"Did you see anything?" Benny asked his brother.

Henry shook his head. "The Eagles pitcher seems okay. Nothing weird about the way he's throwing."

The score was nearly even by the sixth inning. The Eagles led by one point and were up at bat. So far the game appeared to be normal.

Coach Jenkins walked over to the batboy and pulled out a bat for the first hitter. The girl swung it tentatively a few times, then nodded. The bat was okay for her.

Henry knew this girl wasn't much of a hitter. She'd been struck out easily in earlier innings.

Brandon stood on the pitcher's mound.

He swung his arm, then threw the ball. The girl's bat contacted the ball. It arced over the diamond. *Wham!* The ball hit the wooden fence. A home run for the Eagles!

The girl high-fived her other teammates.

"Wow!" exclaimed Benny. "She's good!"

Henry frowned. "Maybe she just got lucky."

But he couldn't say that about the second and third and fourth home runs. Player after player hit line drives right into the fence! They couldn't *all* be lucky, he realized.

"They're either a really good team," said Henry, "or there's something going on. I just can't tell what it is."

The next batter who came up seemed reluctant. From her seat in the grandstand, Violet watched the sandy-haired boy carefully. He took the bat that the coach handed him. *Why was the coach handing out the bats instead of the batboy?* she wondered.

The boy took an open stance and waited for Brandon's pitch. He let the first ball go by. And the second. On the third pitch, he swung and missed. Violet could see Coach Jenkins frown.

On Brandon's next pitch, the boy stepped into the swing, and *crack!* the ball went flying into center field. The ball slammed into the boards.

The sandy-haired boy ran the bases rather halfheartedly, Violet thought. When he reached home, he walked up to the coach. They talked, then the boy gathered his things and left the park.

"He just quit the game," said Violet, surprised.

"Looks like it," Mr. Soper agreed. "Maybe he's sick. Why else would a player quit when his team is winning?"

At the beginning of the next inning, Coach Jenkins came into the bleachers to where Violet was sitting.

"Are you Violet Alden?" he asked her.

"Yes," she replied, wondering what the man wanted.

"Your sister, Jessie, said you are a good ballplayer. Our left fielder just went home sick. And we don't have any substitutes.

Would you like to play with us?" He grinned, adding, "We're winning, you know."

"Well . . ." Then Violet realized this was a good opportunity. With two Aldens working on the inside, there was a better chance to find out if the Eagles were cheating. "Yes," she said. "It sounds like fun."

As she put on an Eagles T-shirt, Violet noticed it was Jessie's turn to bat. Once more Coach Jenkins took a bat from the batboy and gave it to Jessie to test.

Jessie swung the bat tentatively, then held it out straight. The bat seemed fine, not too heavy. She hit a good one deep in the outfield, but it was not a home run.

During a time-out, Jessie murmured to Violet, "I'm glad you're on the team. I can't tell what the Eagles are doing to cheat. Or even if they are cheating. You can help."

"I'll try," said Violet.

It was her turn to bat. She hit a single. It was funny, but only she and Jessie hadn't hit home runs. Were the other players that good?

All too soon, the game was over. The hard-hitting Eagles had won.

After the Eagles had left, Emily jogged over to Jessie. "The last game on Friday is the tie breaker. If we lose that game, we lose the championship."

"But if you win, you'll win the championship," Jessie said.

Henry and Benny joined them.

Brandon walked up, his glove hanging off the end of a bat. "It's important for us to go out winning," he said. "Because after Friday we can't play anymore."

"We still have two days," Henry reminded everyone. "The ballpark could be saved in two days. It's not impossible."

Two days isn't much time, Violet thought.

As she turned, she saw a familiar face behind the batting cage. It was the sandy-haired boy who had quit the team. He motioned for her to come over.

"I thought you went home sick," Violet said to him.

"I was supposed to," said the boy. "My name is Eric. Did you take my position?"

Violet nodded. "Right in the middle of the game."

"I think you should know something," Eric said. "It's about — "

Just then Coach Jenkins loomed over them.

"Eric!" he boomed. "How's that stomachache?"

"Oh, it still hurts," Eric said quickly. "I was just going home. I wanted to see if we won."

"We did," said the coach. "Violet here did a fine job of filling in for you. Will you be back for the championship game on Friday?"

"Uh — no," stammered Eric. "I don't think I'll be better by then."

"Let me walk you to the clubhouse," Coach Jenkins said. "You can collect the rest of your things."

As the coach led him across the field, Eric flashed a desperate glance over his shoulder. Violet knew he was trying to give her a message. It must be something important.

But how could she find out what it was?

CHAPTER 5

The Woman in Purple

After the game, the Aldens went back to the inn. Everyone was disappointed because the Half Moons had lost.

The innkeeper, Bud Towers, noticed the long faces as he served a lunch of turkey salad and watermelon slices. "Looks like our team didn't win today."

"Nope," answered Benny.

"How about if we do a little sightseeing?" Grandfather suggested.

"Where are we going?" Benny wanted to know.

"To someplace special," was Grandfather's mysterious answer.

When they had finished eating, they all got in the station wagon and drove south. Grandfather pulled the car into the parking lot of a strange house.

Violet stared at it as they all climbed out. "It looks like it belongs in a fairy tale," she murmured.

The house had pointed roof lines and odd gables. Ivy clung to the old bricks and stonework. Diamond-shaped windows in witch's-hat dormers overlooked a garden.

Benny had never seen a house like this. "I want to live here!" he exclaimed. Then he remembered his own wonderful house in Greenfield. "But I won't ever leave you, Grandfather."

James Alden laughed. "It's okay, Benny. Everyone is enchanted with Washington Irving's home."

"Is that who lived here?" asked Henry. "I've read some of his stories."

"So have I," Jessie chimed in. "*The Legend of Sleepy Hollow.* And *Rip Van Winkle.*"

They walked inside and joined a tour group already in progress. The guide told them the story of Rip Van Winkle, the man who fell asleep for twenty years.

"Boy!" Benny commented. "I bet he was really hungry when he woke up!"

Everyone in the group laughed.

But the listeners were spellbound as the guide recited the tale of the little men Rip Van Winkle found bowling in the mountains and how Rip fell asleep for twenty years. When Rip went back home, nobody knew him and the town had changed.

After the story, the Aldens walked along a wooded trail that led them to the Hudson.

"The river is at its widest here," Grandfather remarked. "It's magnificent, isn't it?"

The children enjoyed the awesome view of gray-blue water tipped with whitecaps and dotted with boats.

Then they climbed back up the trail to the car. It was such a nice day, Grandfather drove around until he found a deli with outdoor tables. The turkey salad and watermelon at the inn had been good, but they decided they needed a little something "to fill up the corners," as Grandfather quipped.

They ordered baskets of fried onion rings and nachos to share, and sodas.

Jessie turned slightly to see the other diners: Someone had caught her eye. Two tables over, she saw a man who looked familiar. It took her a second to recognize Mike Percy, the Half Moons coach, without his blue baseball jersey on. Today he wore slacks and a green-striped shirt.

A dark-haired woman sat with him. She wore a purple dress and shoes. Even her purse was purple. Jessie guessed she liked that color a lot.

Grandfather noticed the couple, too. "Why, there's Beverly Percy. That must be her husband, Mike."

"It is," said Jessie. "I mean, that's the coach. Who's the lady?"

"Mrs. Percy is the town council member who started the movement to tear down the ballpark," Grandfather replied.

Violet took a second glance at the woman. Mrs. Percy was pretty, with shiny dark hair and blue eyes. But she didn't smile. She seemed angry about something her husband was telling her.

Just then the Aldens' food came. Grandfather passed around the onion rings and divided the cheesy nachos on small plates.

Henry dipped an onion ring in spicy sauce. He was sitting with his back to the Percys but was closest to their table. When the wind blew just right, he could hear parts of their conversation.

". . . got the council members right where I want them . . ." said a harsh female voice.

That has to be Mrs. Percy, Henry thought.

"They vote the day after tomorrow," said Mike Percy. "I hope you're right — "

"I'm always right," Beverly Percy snapped. "Just keep looking for that . . ." The wind snatched away the rest of her sentence.

Henry strained to hear more, but a noisy party of six claimed the table between the Aldens and the Percys.

"They're leaving," Violet said. "I think they're coming this way!"

Grandfather's chair scraped as he stood. "Hello, Mrs. Percy. How nice to see you here."

"Yes," said Mrs. Percy coolly. Her tone said she wasn't pleased to see him at all. "Are these your grandchildren?" She looked sharply at the Alden children.

"They are indeed," said James Alden. "This is Henry, Jessie, Violet, and Benny."

"Would you like an onion ring?" Benny offered.

"No, thanks." Beverly Percy smiled, but it seemed fake, Violet thought.

"We've already met," Mike Percy said quickly. "At the ballpark. Violet and Jessie are pinch-hitting — "

"We must go," interrupted Mrs. Percy. She gave the Aldens a last once-over before leaving in a cloud of strong-smelling perfume.

Jessie thought she recognized the perfume. A saleswoman had once given her a sample in a department store. It was called

Purple Passion, Jessie recalled. Even the woman's fragrance was purple!

When Grandfather left to pay the check, Jessie remarked, "Not very friendly, was she?"

"Not at all," Henry agreed.

The next day Benny leaped out of bed. "Come on, Henry!" he told his older brother. "We don't want to be late!"

"I'm up," Henry said. "I'll be ready in two minutes. We still have to eat breakfast."

"Okay, but hurry!"

The previous day the Aldens had taken a walk around the outside of the old factory. Carl Soper had been there, pruning some bushes. He told them he tried to take care of the old place, even though nobody paid him. And he offered to show the children the inside the next day. They had eagerly agreed to come back.

Now, eager to get back to the factory, the children quickly ate their breakfast of carrot muffins, fresh-squeezed orange juice, and sausage patties. Grandfather left for a meeting, and they walked quickly to the old building. Carl and Emily Soper were waiting for them at the entrance.

Carl jingled a ring of keys. "Good morning," he said. "Ever been inside an abandoned hat factory?"

"No, sir," Violet replied. "We're very excited."

"Well, there isn't much to see." Carl fitted a key into the lock. "I still have keys because I'm the last long-term employee. And I clean up the outside every now and then."

The door swung outward on creaking hinges. Even though it was daytime, the factory was dim inside. Violet wasn't so sure she wanted to take this tour now.

"It's okay," Emily reassured her. "I've been in here a zillion times. Nothing will bother you."

What about that ghost? Jessie wanted to ask. Of course, she didn't believe in ghosts. But Danny Jenkins had said the factory was haunted. The Aldens had seen a mysterious light in the windows with their own eyes.

Carl led them into a large dusty room. Long worktables stood in rows, covered with more dust. Rectangular and square outlines marked the floor and tables.

"That's where the equipment used to be," Carl explained. "When the factory closed, they sold all the machinery. This is the room where I worked."

Benny sneezed from the dust. "What was your job?"

"I was a blocker," Carl replied. "I took the hats that were just made and steamed them into shape. Turned up the brims, rounded the crowns, that sort of thing."

"Gramps was a great blocker," Emily said. "He was the best."

Carl smiled sadly at Emily. "That was all a long time ago." He moved down the hall to another room.

This room was much smaller and just as dusty. Benches were pulled up to a plain table. The walls were lined with small wooden doors.

"Our break room," explained Carl. "This was where we stored our lunches and coats. We ate in here when it was too cold to go outside."

He walked over to a long row of narrow wooden lockers against the wall and opened one. Each locker was labeled with heavy printed initials, faded to gray on stiff paper, slotted into a small frame near the top of its wooden door. Carl slowly ran his finger over the initials C.S. "My old locker," he said.

Henry wandered around the room, trying to imagine what it was like working in this factory many years ago. Sunlight streamed in through the dirty, broken window. The men would have been sitting around the table with their bologna sandwiches and laughing at one another's jokes. It was a shame the place had been closed down.

"Tomorrow is our last game," Emily told Jessie and Violet. Emily looked worried.

"I know," said Violet. "We'll catch the Eagles cheating while they're playing." At least, she hoped they would.

Benny was opening and closing locker doors, looking inside each one. Inside one locker was a pair of old, worn-out boots, in another a ragged work shirt hung on a

hook. It seemed every locker had some scrap of paper or small reminder of the worker who had left it years ago.

"Hey, look at this," Benny called.

Everyone ran over and crowded around Benny.

"What is it?" asked Emily.

"See?" Benny pointed to the pair of faint initials framed in brass at the top of a locker door.

H.S.

Carl drew in his breath. "This must have been the locker of Herman Soper, my uncle. Good work! I never really knew where it was." He was delighted with Benny's find.

"Wow! But . . . your uncle worked here long before you did," said Jessie. "And plenty of other workers passed through this factory after he left. You think his locker was never used again?"

"Maybe nobody wanted to use the locker of the 'cheater,' " Carl said. He shook his head sadly.

"Maybe nobody used it but somebody sure cleaned it out, though," said Benny.

Benny stood on tiptoe to peer into the shelf at the top of the locker. "No old magazines, no book of matches . . . and look. . . ."

"I see what you mean," said Henry, peering into the locker. The locker's shelf was crooked and it had been knocked that way recently. The wood where the shelf had been attached to the locker was fresh and clean, unlike the dark wood of the rest of the locker.

"Are you suggesting Home Run Herman's locker has been searched?" Emily murmured. "You guys really *are* detectives. I bet you will find out the truth about Herman and about the Eagles' home run streak, too."

Jessie glanced at Violet, Henry, and Benny. They couldn't let Emily and her grandfather down.

But this doubleheader mystery was far from being solved. And they only had two more days.

CHAPTER 6

The Ghost Returns

When they finished touring the abandoned factory, the Alden children, Carl, and Emily walked back to the ball-park.

Right away, Violet noticed a white truck pulled up alongside the curb. Carl Soper saw the truck at the same time.

"Who are those guys?" asked Violet.

A man squinted through an instrument mounted on a tripod that looked something like a camera. Way across the field another man stood holding a pole.

"Surveyors," said Carl. "The first man is looking through something called a level transit. The man with the pole is called a rodman. His rod has marks on it that the surveyor uses to measure the boundaries of a piece of property."

"Why are they here?" Jessie wanted to know.

"Good question," said Carl, his face grim. "The town council doesn't vote until tomorrow afternoon about tearing down the ballpark. Somebody hired this crew a little ahead of schedule, if you ask me."

"Maybe *she* did." Benny pointed toward the grandstand.

Sitting on the bottom bleacher was Beverly Percy. Today she wore a purple flowered top over purple slacks. She was smiling as she watched the men working.

"The nerve of that woman!" Carl stalked over to the grandstand. Emily and the Aldens followed.

Mrs. Percy watched their approach. "Hello, Carl," she said. "How are you?"

"I was fine until I saw these surveyors," Carl replied. "Did you hire them?"

She nodded. "I thought it was in the town's best interest to get the ball rolling. The sooner we get rid of this reminder of Pikesville's bad times, the sooner we can rebuild the town into a place people will want to visit and make their home."

"Very pretty speech," Carl said evenly. "I'm sure you've got all the council members convinced, but it doesn't wash with me. You have no right to have the ballpark surveyed until the council has voted."

Mrs. Percy stood, as if dismissing Carl. "I understand why you are bitter, Carl. It was your relative who brought bad luck on Pikesville. Too bad you share his name. But Pikesville can wipe out those old memories. And it will."

"But the council doesn't vote until tomorrow," Henry said. "Why are you so sure everyone will vote to tear down the ballpark?"

Beverly Percy gave him and the other Aldens a sharp glance. "You children don't even live here. Why don't you mind your own business?"

"Their grandfather was asked to advise the council," Carl reminded her. "As I recall, you're an outsider yourself. You and your husband only moved here six months ago."

Mrs. Percy made a big show of checking her watch. "I really have better things to do than chitchat with you." She left the grandstand in a huff.

"Pssst!" came a voice.

Out of the corner of her eye, Violet caught a motion underneath the bleacher to the side. She looked down between the weathered boards.

It was Eric, the player who had quit the Eagles! But when he saw Mrs. Percy striding in front of the grandstand, he scrambled away before Violet could call out to him.

"That boy was here," she told the others. "Under the seats."

"What boy?" asked Jessie.

"Eric, the one I replaced on the team," replied Violet. "See, there he goes. He's running away."

Sure enough, the sandy-haired boy was sprinting out of the park.

"What was he doing under the bleachers?" asked Emily. "Why didn't he come sit with us?"

"I think he's trying to tell me something," Violet guessed. "But he seems afraid."

Emily was still puzzled. "Why? Of what?"

Violet shook her head. "I don't know."

If only she could speak to him!

The kids practiced throwing and catching with Emily until lunchtime. They had the ballpark to themselves; no Eagles were around. Then Emily stuck her mitt and ball in her backpack.

"Can't you store your things in the clubhouse?" Jessie asked. She had been wanting to get in there ever since the first day, when she had seen Coach Jenkins switch the bat Emily had chosen for another.

"I can, but then I don't have them with me later if I want to play catch with

Gramps. The clubhouse is always locked," Emily told them.

"Your grandfather has a lot of keys," Benny said.

"Not to the clubhouse," said Emily. "Only the two coaches have keys. I need to go home and fix Gramps's lunch," she said. "See you guys tomorrow for the game." She held up crossed fingers.

"Don't worry," Henry told her. "We still have time to work on saving the ballpark and catch the cheaters."

"I'm not worried," Emily said with a grin. "I believe you guys are good luck."

They watched her leave, backpack slung over her shoulder.

"I hope she's right," said Jessie.

The children walked back to the Half Moon Inn. Grandfather was in a luncheon meeting, but Bud Towers handed Jessie a huge wicker hamper.

"I fixed you kids a picnic," the innkeeper said. "If you go down Bolton Street, you will come to a park along the river.

There are tables under the trees. It's very nice."

"Great idea," said Jessie, hefting the basket. "Thanks."

Bolton Street wasn't far from the inn. From there, it was a short hike to the park. Old oak trees sheltered wooden picnic tables. Well-tended flower beds bordered the pebbled pathways. Just beyond, the Hudson River flowed in a broad silvery ribbon.

"This is cool," said Benny. "Let's eat over there. It's closest to the water." He ran and claimed the large table.

Jessie began unpacking the wicker hamper. "Mr. Towers thought of everything. Even a tablecloth."

She gave Henry the old quilt tucked around the food. Henry spread the quilt on the table. Violet passed around plates and napkin-bundled flatware.

Soon the table was spread with plastic containers of fried chicken, rolls still warm from the oven, potato salad, baked beans, fresh fruit, and gingersnaps. A thermos held lemonade.

The children ate heartily.

"Yum," Violet commented.

Benny reached for another drumstick. "I'm always hungrier when I'm outside."

"You're pretty hungry indoors, too," Henry teased. "But I know what you mean. Eating in the fresh air is more fun."

Jessie was snapping the lid back on the chicken when she noticed two men. They had just sat down at a distant picnic table.

"There's Mike Percy," she said. "Isn't that Coach Jenkins with him?"

The others turned to look.

"That's them, all right," said Henry. "On the ballpark they act like they can't stand each other. I wonder why they seem so buddy-buddy now."

The coaches were talking intently. Coach Jenkins glanced around every so often, as if he were afraid of being overheard.

"They're acting weird," remarked Violet. "Like they've got a big secret or something."

Just then, Coach Jenkins noticed the

Aldens. He got up and hurried away. Mike Percy followed a moment later.

"Well, *that* was strange," Jessie said. "So far we've run into a lot of suspicious characters on this case, like Coach Jenkins and the Percys, and maybe even Danny. *Now* they're getting together!"

"But we have no clues," Henry pronounced solemnly. "And no leads."

That evening, the children took their usual after-dinner stroll to the ballpark. In the fading twilight, the factory looked spookier than ever.

Suddenly two lights flickered in a lower window.

Benny gasped. "The ghost!"

"There are no ghosts," Jessie told him. But the wavery lights were scary. If it wasn't a ghost, then what was it?

"Look," said Henry.

Two figures flitted across the windows.

"The ghost has returned," Henry observed. "And he brought a friend."

"People are in there," Violet said. "Maybe it's Carl and Emily."

But at that moment Carl and Emily Soper came up the walk.

When he saw the children's faces, Carl said, "What's the matter?"

"Some people are in the factory," Benny said. "At least, we *think* they're people."

But the lights had vanished. Once more the factory was cloaked in darkness.

"We'd better check it out," said Carl. He produced his key ring and headed for the front door.

Unlocking it, Carl switched on the flashlight he always wore on his belt. With Carl and Henry leading the way, they crept inside.

Carl's beam swept from side to side.

"The coast is clear," Henry announced. "Whoever was here is gone."

"They didn't leave by the front door," said Carl. "It was locked. So how did these people get in and out without us seeing them?"

Benny didn't want to think about the answer to that question.

They clattered down the empty corridor. The doors were closed, as Carl had left them.

All but one.

This room contained old wooden file cabinets. The drawers of the cabinets stood open. Yellowed papers were scattered all over the floor.

"This is the file room," Carl said. "Old records were kept here. Papers that nobody is interested in anymore."

Two people were interested, thought Henry. The "ghosts" were clearly hunting for something.

Jessie sniffed. A sickening sweet smell hung in the stale air. She knew that perfume.

It was Purple Passion.

CHAPTER 7

Henry's Discovery

"Take me out to the ball game!" Benny sang as he skipped along with his brother and sisters to the ballpark.

It was Friday, the day of the championship game. Mockingbirds sang from the old oaks that grew in the vacant lot next to the ballpark.

"It seems a shame to tear this down," Jessie said. "All they need to do is mow the grass and paint the bleachers. It's right in the middle of town and most kids can walk to it."

"It's up to the town council," Henry pointed out. "They'll vote this afternoon. From the way Grandfather talked at breakfast, it looks as if they will vote to turn it into a parking lot. Nobody has found any reason to make it a historical landmark. Quite the opposite. They want to forget its history."

"I bet the factory 'ghosts' know something," said Jessie. "We didn't see the Percys last night, but we know they were there. That was definitely Mrs. Percy's perfume."

Benny nodded. "Don't forget about Coach Jenkins. He's friends with Mr. Percy."

"He may not be," Henry sighed. "They were just talking yesterday."

"We have to find out if the Eagles are cheating first," Violet reminded them. "We'll have to think about mystery number two later."

"Right," said Jessie. "You and I will stay on the Eagles' team."

"And Benny and I will watch from the sidelines," said Henry.

"Like hawks!" Benny added.

Violet glanced around the empty street. "I hope Eric comes back today. Maybe I can talk to him and find out what he knows."

"We don't know where he lives," Jessie said. "So we can't go ask him."

Henry led the way into the ballpark, where the players were pulling on gear or practicing. "We can't count on Eric showing up. It's up to us to find out if the Eagles are cheating."

On the field, Violet and Jessie joined the Eagles team in their dugout. Benny wished them luck, then found Emily's grandfather sitting in his usual place. He looked to see if any Eagles were watching, then he waved and Carl Soper waved back.

The coaches were huddled with their teams. Benny could feel tension in the air. This wasn't just another game.

Then the umpire called, "Play ball!" and the action started.

Emily's team was batting first again. Danny, the Eagles' pitcher, rolled his shoulders and smacked the ball into his well-worn glove.

Brandon was up at bat. Danny threw the pitch. Brandon hit the ball into right field. The Eagles right fielder was the girl who missed a lot of balls. She fumbled this one. Brandon raced to first and was safe.

From her position in center field, Jessie was glad the game was starting well for the Half Moons.

They scored two runs in the first inning. But in the second inning, the scoreboard changed dramatically when the Eagles batted. Just like in the final inning of the last game, the Eagles batted home run after home run.

"It's like they have a magic bat," Benny said to Henry from behind the batting cage. He'd been thinking about magic lately, since he had heard the story of Rip Van Winkle.

Henry stared at him. "Benny! I think you've hit the ball out of the park!"

"Me?" Benny was confused. "I'm not even playing!"

"It's an expression. You gave me an idea!" Henry clung to the wire of the cage, staring intently at each of the Eagles players. "See that girl coming up now? She plays right field. She's not a very strong hitter."

But the girl whacked the ball high. It didn't hit the fence but came so close that the Half Moons outfielders couldn't run over and throw it in fast enough. Another home run.

"That was good," commented Benny.

"Too good," Henry said suspiciously. He thought he'd figured out the answer to this mystery. Now he needed proof.

"Everybody is hitting a home run," Benny observed. "Except Jessie and Violet."

"You're right," said Henry. "We need to talk to them."

Henry waited until the inning was over and the glum Half Moons team was switching places with the Eagles.

Henry and Benny ran along the foul line, beckoning to their sisters.

Jessie and Violet came over.

"What is it?" asked Jessie. "We only have a second."

"The bat you're using," Henry asked. "Is there something funny about it?"

Jessie shrugged. "It seems okay."

"You guys aren't hitting home runs," Henry said. "But the others are."

"Henry's right," Violet said to Jessie.

"Are they using the same bat as you are?" Henry asked.

"Jessie and Violet!" Danny called from the pitcher's mound. "Places!"

"I think the other players are handed a different bat," said Jessie. "But I don't know for sure. We've got to go."

When the girls were back in the outfield, Henry said to Benny, "Let's go over to the clubhouse. I have a hunch."

The game was well under way again. They walked quickly to the old clubhouse. Nobody paid attention to them.

"We're in luck," Henry said. "The door is open! Let's hope there are two of them."

"Two of what?" Benny asked.

Henry poked his head in the door. He drew in a quick breath when he saw a lone bat leaning against the wall. It was within his reach.

He stretched his hand out and took the bat.

Benny watched his brother bounce the end of the bat in his hand. "What are you doing?" he wanted to know.

"Feel this." Henry handed the bat to Benny.

Benny nearly dropped it. "It's so light!"

"This is the Eagles' secret weapon," Henry declared. "They use corked bats."

"What?" asked Benny.

"Remember when Grandfather said you could eat a lot because you have a hollow leg?" Henry said.

"Yeah."

"Well, the Eagles win because they use hollow bats." Henry examined the end of the bat. "See this?"

Benny looked carefully. "There's a lighter circle on the end."

"That's where the bat was cored," Henry said. "Someone drilled into the end, removed the wood, and put in something

lighter, like cork. Then they covered it with a plug of wood."

Benny touched the tip of the bat. "How would this make people hit home runs?"

"A lighter bat is a faster bat," Henry explained. "You can swing it easier. That makes the fat part of the bat — the part that hits the ball — move through the strike zone faster. And the cork makes the ball really bounce off the bat."

Now Benny understood. "So even if you weren't a very good hitter, you could hit homers with this bat."

"It's against the rules," Henry said. "We have to let the umpire and Coach Percy know as soon as possible. There's probably another bat just like this and that's what the Eagles are using today. This is the spare."

"Coach Jenkins will have to confess," said Benny. "I bet the whole thing was his idea."

"Let's go," Henry said.

As Benny leaned into the clubhouse to pull the door shut, he saw an old glass-fronted cabinet filled with old tarnished trophies, its glass doors cracked and dusty. He slid one open and peered inside. Photographs of baseball players in old-timey uniforms, faded pennants, and posters announcing games were pasted on the inside back wall. He stepped into the clubhouse to get a closer look.

"Hurry," Henry told him. "We don't want the Half Moons to lose."

Before he turned, Benny found what he was looking for on the picture wall. It was an old photograph of the Pikesville Grays. Next to it was a list of the players' names. Benny checked the list, looking for Herman's. . . . Herbert Smith — no, that wasn't it. . . . There it was: Herman Washburn Soper. Benny hadn't been looking for a middle name and almost missed it. An idea began to form in Benny's head. But he didn't have time to think it through. Henry was rushing toward the bleachers.

In the stands, Henry handed the bat to Emily's grandfather.

Carl Soper hefted the bat. "Corked," he said. "Where did you find it?"

"In the clubhouse," Benny responded.

"I bet there's two of these bats," said Carl. "And I bet the Eagles are using the other one right now. You kids did good work. I think we should call a time-out."

The boys followed Carl down the stands and over to the umpire. He showed the bat to the umpire, who called loudly for a time-out.

Jessie wondered what was going on. Henry, Benny, and Carl Soper stood with the umpire. They were all staring at a bat.

Violet came over. "What is it?"

Jessie shook her head. "I don't know. But I think something is about to happen. Let's find out." She and Violet moved closer to the action.

The umpire signaled to the coaches. When Coach Jenkins saw the bat Henry had found, his face turned bright red.

"Get the other one!" Carl Soper demanded. "And don't pretend you don't have it."

Angry, Coach Jenkins snapped his fingers at the batboy. The boy brought over a bat and reluctantly handed it to the umpire.

Henry could see the second bat had a lighter-colored circle on the end, the tell-tale plug. It, too, had been drilled and filled with cork.

"You've been cheating all along!" Carl Soper accused Coach Jenkins. "You couldn't beat us fairly, so you decided to cheat!"

Coach Jenkins threw his hat to the ground. "Who needs this? I volunteered my summers for years, and for what?" He turned and left the infield.

"The coach just quit," said Violet. "In the middle of the game!"

Carl Soper shook his head in disgust.

"The teams can still play, can't they?" asked Benny.

Mike Percy tapped his wristwatch. "I'm afraid not. Not after today. The town council will vote at one o'clock. As soon as they do, nobody will be able to use the ballpark."

The Aldens stared at one another.

They had run out of time!

CHAPTER 8

Game Over!

"The Eagles forfeited the game by cheating, but it's not the same as us *really* winning," Emily said, dejected, "and it's not going to change anyone's mind about Home Run Herman *or* the ballpark."

"We're really sorry," Benny told her.

"It's not your fault," said Emily. "At least you guys found how the Eagles were cheating."

"But not in time," Henry said.

Players were leaving the field, shoulders slumped. Danny Jenkins skulked off with his older brother.

"Technically, we didn't lose, because they cheated," Mike Percy told Emily. "Too bad we can't replay the entire season."

Jessie thought the coach seemed awfully cheerful, considering his team had lost the chance to win their last championship.

"Maybe you kids can play soccer instead," Mike said breezily. "I've heard a rumor the town might build a field out by the highway. Well, I'd better go. I'm meeting my wife for a quick bite before the council meeting. It's at one."

Jessie's heart thumped. How could they possibly save the ballpark by one o'clock? They had hardly started on *that* mystery.

Carl Soper must have read her mind. "I'm going to miss this place," he said, gazing around the outfield. "I've spent many Saturdays here, playing or coaching or watching games. It just won't be the same."

"I know," sighed Emily. "And I don't believe anybody will build a new ballpark for us. They're more interested in turning the factory into a mini-mall."

The Alden children, Carl Soper, and

Emily wandered slowly around the foul line. Brandon joined them.

"If only we had won," said Brandon. "Then at least we'd have the trophy."

"Nobody won," Emily commented. "So nobody gets the trophy." Suddenly she turned to her grandfather. "The clubhouse will be torn down, too, won't it? What will happen to all the old stuff inside, like our old trophies and the photographs?"

Before Carl could answer, footsteps thudded behind them.

Violet whirled to see Eric, the shy boy who had been hiding under the bleachers.

"Eric!" she exclaimed. "What are you doing here? The game is over."

"I know," he said. "I saw your brothers hand over that special bat to the umpire."

"You knew about the bats?" Henry asked.

Eric nodded. "Not at first. But then I thought it was funny that Coach Jenkins always made us use a certain bat. We couldn't pick our own."

"Could you tell it had been tampered with?" asked Carl.

"This is my first year playing ball," Eric replied. "I wasn't sure there was anything wrong with the bat. Once I took another bat by mistake. I could tell it was heavier."

Jessie had a question. "Did you hit home runs?"

"Yeah," said Eric. "And I'm not very good. I finally figured it was the special bat making me hit better. So I quit the team."

"Is that what you wanted to tell me the other day?" Violet queried. "And yesterday when you were under the bleachers?"

Eric looked embarrassed. "Sorry I ran off. I got nervous. Yeah, I did want to mention the bats. But there's something else I think you should know. About the ballpark."

Now Emily was interested. "What about the ballpark?"

Eric glanced around, then froze.

The others looked in the same direction.

Mike and Beverly Percy were crossing the infield. Beverly carried a large white paper sack. They sat down on the bottom bleacher in the grandstand and began taking wrapped sandwiches and drinks from the bag.

"Strange to choose this place to have lunch," said Henry. "Considering she wants to tear it down."

Eric became nervous. "Can we get out of here?"

Jessie knew he was afraid of the Percys. "Sure. Let's all get something to eat."

Carl Soper told them about a little eatery nearby called The Doghouse. "They serve the best chili dogs in town."

"Mmmmm," said Benny. "Let's hurry before they run out!"

Emily laughed. "It's a restaurant, Benny! They aren't supposed to run out of food!"

The Doghouse *was* small. But the food was cheap and good. Everyone got chili dogs, potato chips, and soft drinks to go.

Then they went to the park along the river. Under the shade of an oak tree, the group claimed a wide picnic table and unpacked their lunches.

Benny bit into his chili dog, loaded with meat, beans, cheese, onions, and mustard. "This is the best thing I've ever eaten," he declared.

"Until tonight at dinner," Jessie teased. "Then you'll say *that* is the best thing you've ever eaten."

Violet wanted to know what Eric had to say. "Can you talk now?" she asked him.

Eric wiped mustard off his chin. "Yeah. Those guys aren't around."

"You mean the Percys," said Henry.

Eric nodded. "After a game last week, I forgot my jersey. My mom said she needed to wash it, so I went back. I had left it in the clubhouse. Everybody had gone home except the coaches. When I walked up to the clubhouse, I heard them talking."

"What were they saying?" asked Benny.

"Coach Percy was telling my coach, 'You *must* find it!' " answered Eric.

Jessie took a thoughtful sip of her soda. "Find what? What were they talking about?"

"Some kind of paper," Eric replied.

"Coach Jenkins said he had been looking for it every night. In the factory."

Jessie looked at Henry. "The ghost that Danny told me about. It was his brother! Coach Jenkins was 'haunting' the old factory, looking for something."

"Except one night there were two ghosts," Violet reminded her. "Mr. and Mrs. Percy. They were looking for something in the file room."

"I bet they were all looking for that paper," Benny put in. Then he asked Eric, "But what does this have to do with the ballpark?"

"When Mr. Percy and Coach Jenkins were in the clubhouse," Eric went on, "I heard Coach Jenkins say, 'You don't need it. As long as no one else finds it, the ballpark will be torn down anyway.' "

"That's what he said?" Carl queried. "That the ballpark will be torn down anyway?"

Brandon was bewildered. "How could they know that? The meeting isn't until today."

"Good question," stated Henry. "It

sounds like that paper the Percys and Coach Jenkins were looking for is important."

"Do you know about any paper?" Emily asked her grandfather.

Carl Soper shook his head regretfully. "I can't think of anything that might save the ballpark."

"We're missing a piece to the puzzle," Jessie said, nervously chewing her thumbnail. "I bet it's right under our noses."

Benny glanced up at her. But before he could speak, Danny Jenkins came running up to their picnic table.

"Hey!" he greeted the Aldens. "I just saw your grandfather. He said to meet him at the old factory. That's where the town council is meeting to vote."

Without waiting for a reply, Danny ran off.

"That's weird," said Violet. "Wouldn't the town council have their meeting in the town hall?"

"They always have before," said Carl Soper. "Maybe they want to look at the factory one last time before the vote."

"We'd better go," Henry said, hastily picking up the trash from their lunch. "We don't want to miss the vote."

Both Eric and Brandon said they had to go home and the rest of the group hurried back to the old hat factory. Carl Soper went up to the front doors and tried the handle.

"It's locked!" he declared. "Nobody is in this building."

"Danny led us here on purpose!" Jessie exclaimed. "He wanted us out of the way when the council voted!"

Henry checked his watch. "We still have time to make it."

Everyone pelted down the steps and followed the cracked walkway around the factory. Jessie, who was in the lead, saw two people slip into the clubhouse.

She held up a hand to silence the others. "The Percys just went into the clubhouse," she informed them.

Emily frowned. "I thought Mrs. Percy was at the town meeting."

"This looks very suspicious," Henry said. "Maybe the game isn't over yet!"

"Let's find out what those two are up to," said Carl.

Everyone rushed to the clubhouse.

The door was open. Mrs. Percy's voice floated out.

"Well, it's not here, either," they heard her say. "Did you tell Jenkins we were coming back for one more look?"

"No, but things look good," came her husband's voice. "Everything is going according to plan."

"I just wish we had found that letter," said Mrs. Percy.

Benny got so excited he forgot to keep his voice down. "I think I know where the letter is," he cried.

Just then Beverly Percy stepped out and saw them. She looked very angry.

CHAPTER 9

Mrs. Pettibone's Letter

"What are you people doing here?" demanded Mrs. Percy.

"Anyone can come here," Carl Soper returned.

"We should be going," Mike Percy said, clearly nervous. "The council meeting will be starting."

He and his wife started to leave.

Benny tugged on Carl Soper's sleeve. When the older man bent down, Benny whispered something in his ear.

"Isn't the meeting in the old factory?"

Henry asked the Percys. "That's what Danny Jenkins told us."

"I don't know what you're talking about," said Mrs. Percy. "Why would the council meet in that run-down old place? Now, if you'll excuse us — "

"We think somebody ordered Danny to get us out of the way," Jessie concluded. "So we won't upset the vote."

Mrs. Percy snorted. "How ridiculous. You're just children. You can't vote!"

"No, but these children can find out things," said Carl. "Like Benny here."

Jessie was surprised. "Benny, what did you find?"

"Nothing yet, but I think it's in the factory, in Herman's locker," Benny said. "I'm not sure what it is, but I think it's important."

"But I looked there!" Mrs. Percy blurted out. Mike Percy stiffened.

"Please let the boy show us what he's thinking of," Carl Soper said to them.

Reluctantly, the couple followed Benny and the others to the factory.

Once inside, Benny walked straight to the break room where the old workers' lockers lined the walls. He passed right by the locker labeled H.S. and looked at all the others carefully.

"I bet this is it!" he cried in front of one of the lockers. "I bet what they are looking for is in here. See, H.W.S. — Herman Washburn Soper. He had a funny middle name, didn't he?"

Everyone was shocked.

"Benny," Jessie asked, "how did you know Herman's middle name was Washburn?"

"I saw it in the clubhouse. On the old team photograph. I started to get the idea about the initials and the lockers, but the idea sort of got stuck. When I heard the Percys talking in the clubhouse about some letter they were looking for, the idea just kind of got unstuck."

"It certainly did!" exclaimed Henry, and they all laughed, all except for the Percys.

"I think we'd better see if anything's in here," Carl Soper said, and he opened the locker. He drew out an old newspaper, laid it carefully on the floor, and peered long and hard into the top shelf and the larger bottom part of the locker. He reached his hand in and ran it carefully up and down the sides. "That seems to be it," he said.

The Percys breathed a sigh of relief.

"Wait," said Carl. "I think I feel something. It seems to be stuck between the shelf and the back of the locker." Slowly he drew his arm out. In his hand was a letter.

Everyone gathered around.

"Who's it to?" Violet wanted to know.

Carl squinted at the faded handwriting. "It's addressed to Herman Soper! And it's dated June 4, 1908! That was the year my uncle disappeared!" Carl Soper said. He turned the envelope over. "Why, it's still sealed!"

Carl's hands shook as he opened the letter. He read the document silently for a while. "Listen: 'Dear Mr. Soper,' it says. 'It has come to my attention that I have unknowingly been the cause of some injustice done to you and I am writing this letter to fix it. I took your name from the newspa-

per. Your address was not reported, but the Pikesville Hat Company was mentioned as your place of employment, so I am directing my letter to you there. Please feel free to forward my letter to your local newspaper so they may print the true story of your generosity. I will guarantee the truth of this letter in person should the paper so wish. But as I plan to leave next month on an extended trip . . .' This is incredible! According to this, Herman didn't throw the game!"

"This is all very interesting, but we need to get to that meeting," Beverly Percy said crisply.

"Not so fast," Carl told her.

Jessie noticed both Percys had become jittery since Benny's discovery. They acted like they knew something about this mysterious letter.

Carl took a deep breath. "It was written by Mrs. Daisy Pettibone from Eddington, New York."

"Who is she?" asked Benny.

"She's the lady my uncle stopped to help

on the way to the big game," said Carl Soper, scanning the paper. "It confirms everything Home Run Herman said. He came upon a lady whose Model T was stuck in the mud."

"Model what?" asked Benny.

"The Model T was an early Ford car," answered Henry.

"Automobiles were pretty new in those days," Carl went on. "And roads weren't very good. Mrs. Pettibone asked Herman to push her car out of the ditch. After he helped move her car, she noticed he was rubbing his shoulder. According to the letter, Mrs. Pettibone was in a terrible rush to get home to Eddington. She offered Herman twenty dollars to pay for his assistance. Herman refused. But she insisted and he stuck the bill in his pocket. When he hurried off to the game, he probably forgot about the money."

"Did Mrs. Pettibone go to the game?" asked Emily.

Carl shook his head as he scanned the letter. "No, she got in her car and drove home to the party she was late for. It says here that she didn't know what happened at the game until she got her local newspaper later that week."

"Boy, the news sure was slow in the olden days," Benny commented.

Henry smiled. "Only big cities had daily papers," he said. "Small towns like Pikesville and Eddington had papers that came out once a week."

"It's too bad," Carl Soper remarked. "If Mrs. Pettibone had known sooner, my uncle wouldn't have left town in disgrace."

"Why?" asked Violet.

Carl Soper returned to the letter. "According to this, Mrs. Pettibone was very upset to learn he was accused of throwing the game because he had her twenty dollars in his pocket. She wrote to Herman so he could show the letter to the president of the ball club and the newspaper, and be cleared of any wrongdoing.

"But I don't think he ever received the letter," Carl said sadly. "It was sealed. It was probably delivered after he left town in disgrace."

Mike Percy cleared his throat. "We'd like to hear about old baseball games, but we really have to get to that meeting."

"Yes. The council needs my vote," stated Beverly Percy.

Jessie looked at her. "Why were you in the clubhouse?"

Now Mrs. Percy's tone became frosty. "That is none of your business, young lady." Glancing one last time at the letter Carl Soper held, she turned on her heel and marched out.

Mike Percy was right behind her. The kids heard a car start and drive away. The Percys must have had their car parked on the street behind the clubhouse.

"Those people are strange," Benny commented.

"Not strange," said Henry, an idea forming in his head. "They are very smart."

"How so?" asked Carl.

"The 'ghost' we kept seeing in the old

factory," Henry said. "That was either Jenkins or the Percys. They were all searching for that letter."

"Why would they be hunting for this?" asked Emily.

Now Jessie caught on. "Because it's somehow connected to the ballpark, I bet. The council should know about it."

"The council is going to vote on making this land into a parking lot in ten minutes," Carl Soper announced.

"We've got to get to that meeting!" Violet declared. "Maybe the letter will make a difference in how people vote."

Mr. Soper gave the letter to Benny. "I won't be able to move as fast as you. Now hurry!"

Benny tucked the letter carefully in his pocket. Then he and the other kids sped out of the clubhouse.

"I know a shortcut," Emily told the Aldens.

They dashed across the ballpark and down a side street.

Henry was the fastest runner, but he stayed beside Benny.

The town hall sat in the middle of a green lawn. Revolutionary War cannons flanked the wide steps. The gilded dome glowed like pure gold in the summer sun.

The children flew along the brick walkway and up the granite steps. Henry pulled the heavy double doors open and let Benny enter first.

Benny's sneakers squeaked loudly on the marble floor. Inside, the building was cool and hushed, like a library. He heard voices from the first room on the right. A paneled oak door was propped open.

"In there," Jessie said.

Benny raced to the doorway. He saw men and women sitting around a large wooden table. At one end of the room, Beverly Percy was talking as she stood beside an easel. The drawing on the easel showed a modern parking lot and pretty flowers around the factory building.

"Well, ladies and gentlemen," said Beverly. "Shall we take a vote on this new project?"

Benny wasn't sure what to do. Then he saw Grandfather. At the same time, Grandfather saw him and the others in the doorway behind him.

"Benny!" exclaimed James Alden. "What are you children doing here?"

"I have something to show you," said Benny, handing the letter to his grandfather.

Mrs. Percy's face turned as purple as the dress she had on today. "Pay no attention to that child! He doesn't know anything about my great-aunt's letter!"

CHAPTER 10

Benny's Home Run

Silence fell over the room.

"What did you say?" Emily asked Beverly Percy.

"Nothing," she answered briskly. "Clear these children out so we can get down to business — "

Her husband broke in. "They have the letter, Beverly. We have to tell them."

"Tell us what?" said the man sitting at the head of the table.

"The truth," Jessie stated. Then she added, "We know the Percys have been looking for this letter. Fortunately, our little brother found it in the factory first."

Now James Alden put on his reading glasses and looked at the letter Benny handed him. "It's addressed to Herman Soper."

"Home Run Herman?" said the man at the head of the table. "I'm Paul White," he added, introducing himself to the Alden children, "president of the town council. You say Mr. and Mrs. Percy were looking for this letter?"

Henry nodded. "We saw lights in the old factory. Danny Jenkins told us the factory was haunted. But it was his brother, looking for that paper. The Percys were hunting for it, too."

Mr. White turned to Beverly Percy. "What connection do you have with an old letter addressed to Home Run Herman?"

"It's a long story." Mrs. Percy smiled falsely. "Let's vote first and afterward go have coffee. I'll tell you about the letter then."

"I think now would be better," said

Grandfather. "These children made quite an effort to get the letter here *before* the vote."

In the momentary silence Carl Soper entered the room and with a heavy sigh, Beverly Percy slumped in her chair. "The woman who wrote that letter was my great-aunt, Daisy Pettibone," she began. "I grew up in Eddington, a small town north of here. That's where Aunt Daisy lived, too. I didn't know my great-aunt very well. But when she died, she left me some money."

"When we went through Mrs. Pettibone's belongings, we found a copy of that letter," Mike Percy put in. "Apparently Mrs. Pettibone made and kept copies of most of her correspondence."

"Why was the letter important?" asked Carl Soper.

"It has to do with the ballpark, doesn't it?" guessed Violet.

Beverly shot the kids a dark look. "Yes," she replied. "You see, my aunt had an old newspaper clipping in her files, too. It was about that old baseball game, the one

Home Run Herman supposedly lost on purpose. Mike and I were curious about Pikesville, so we drove down to see the town."

Mike took up the story. "We wanted to make a quick profit. A real estate agent in Eddington told us about the problems in Pikesville and a property that might be coming up for sale."

"What property?" asked Mr. White.

"The ballpark," Beverly Percy answered. "The way we understood it, the ballpark was next to the old factory. We knew you all were thinking about renovating the factory into shops. If we bought the ballpark, we knew we could sell it back to the town at a profit. You'd need that land around the factory."

"So Bev and I moved here," Mike said, taking up the story. "I got a job and became coach of the baseball team. Bev was elected to the town council a few months ago."

"That was part of your scheme," Jessie said. "You got on the council so you could tell people to tear down the ballpark."

"You convinced everyone that the town would be better off without it," Henry added. "Home Run Herman brought shame to Pikesville. If the ballpark was gone, people would forget what happened."

"You kids are pretty smart," Beverly acknowledged. "Yes, I used the old scandal to convince council members to tear the ballpark down. They didn't know Mike and I had an agreement to buy the land."

"But you overlooked one important detail," said Grandfather.

Beverly sighed deeply. "I was hoping you wouldn't bring that up."

"Bring up what?" asked Benny.

"The old factory was declared historical," said James Alden. "If the town could find a good reason to make the ballpark a historical landmark too, it would stay."

Benny was confused. "I don't understand."

"It means there was a good chance that the Percys' sweet deal could be ruined," Henry replied. "The letter from Mrs. Percy's great-aunt proved that Home Run

Herman didn't do anything wrong. Knowing the truth would make people feel good about that old ballpark, and she didn't want that."

"That's right," said Violet.

"If the town found the letter," said Grandfather, "they might keep the ballpark. The Percys would lose their chance to buy the land cheaply and sell it back to the town for a profit. If the land could be made into a parking lot it would be worth a lot more to them."

Mr. White had been studying the letter. Now he passed it to the next council member around the table. "I think this document casts a new light on the situation. Please review it and we'll discuss it."

While Mrs. Pettibone's letter was being examined, the Aldens still had some questions for Mike and Beverly Percy.

"How did you get in the old factory?" Henry asked them. Carl Soper has the only keys."

Beverly shook her head. "That's not true. The town has a set, too. As a member of the town council, I had a right to inspect the old factory. I took the keys and had duplicates made."

"You gave a set to Coach Jenkins," Jessie guessed. "And kept one for yourself. That way you could get into the factory and the clubhouse whenever you wanted."

Mike nodded. "Even though we knew Herman Soper had left Pikesville years ago, the original of Daisy Pettibone's letter might still be around. As it happens, we were looking in the wrong places."

"How did you get out the other night?" Jessie asked the couple. "I smelled Mrs. Percy's perfume, so we knew it was you. But we didn't see you leave."

"Coach Jenkins pried open a back door," Mike explained. "When we heard you coming, we left."

"What about the game?" Emily asked Mike. "Did you know Coach Jenkins was making the Eagles cheat?"

"Yes. Bev and I needed help hunting for that letter. The factory is pretty big and we could only search at night, after work," confessed Mike. "So we asked Coach Jenkins if he'd help. He wanted his team to win the championship. And we figured if the Half Moons started losing all the time, it would be more reason for the council to tear down the old ballpark. I suggested corking a couple of bats."

The council members had finished reviewing the letter.

Mr. White rapped on the table. "I think we've had ample time to reach a decision." He looked long and hard at Mrs. Percy. "I expect your resignation from the town council before this meeting ends. Ladies and gentlemen, let's vote."

Mr. White asked, "Should the ballpark attached to the factory be torn down?"

All the members replied, "No."

"Should the ballpark then be declared a historical property and be restored to its former glory?" Mr. White asked the group.

One by one, the members answered, "Yes."

"Yay!" cried Benny.

Mr. White grinned. "Very good. I'll meet

with the newspaper this afternoon to tell them the truth about Herman Soper. Mrs. Pettibone's letter will be printed, too."

"People will be fascinated to learn an old wrong will finally be righted," said Grandfather. "You will have lots of publicity for the factory renovation."

"You should name it after Herman," Violet suggested.

"That's an excellent idea!" Mr. White agreed. "We'll call the new mini-mall Herman Soper Place. We'll put up a statue of Home Run Herman in the ballpark."

"Are we going to keep the ballpark for sure?" Emily asked eagerly.

"Of course! It'll be a great place to have fairs and other events when you young people aren't playing ball," said Mr. White, "and it's right in town, close to everything."

The Percys were edging toward the door.

"Where are you going?" Henry called loudly.

"Oh. I don't think we're needed here anymore," said Mrs. Percy. "Mike and I have an appointment . . . in another town."

They left in a hurry.

"Good riddance," Carl Soper remarked. Then he turned to his granddaughter with a happy smile. "The Soper name has been cleared at last! We'll never know what happened to Herman, but at least his good name has been restored."

"I wonder where they'll put the statue of Herman," said Benny.

"Maybe by the bleachers," said Violet. "So he can 'watch' all the home runs Emily will hit."

Emily blushed. "You know, Benny," she said, "you hit a home run yourself."

Benny was surprised. "I did? When?"

"When you found the letter and ran to the town hall. You hit a winning run! The ballpark is saved. Gramps and I can't thank you all enough."

"We were glad to help," Violet said, speaking for her brothers and sister.

They had solved the doubleheader case. They'd caught the cheating baseball team and prevented a ballpark from being torn

down. And a local hero would finally be recognized.

While the council members gathered around the children to get the details of the last several days, Benny seemed lost in thought. Grandfather noticed and asked him what was on his mind, and Mr. White turned to listen.

"Well," Benny began slowly, "I like the idea of a statue of Herman in the ballpark, but there is something the ballpark needs much more."

"And what might that be?" asked Mr. White.

"It needs a refreshment stand. The Herman *W.* Soper Refreshment Stand!"

Mr. White clapped Benny on the back.

"A fine idea, Benny!" Mr. White exclaimed. "But maybe we should call it the Benny Alden Refreshment Stand."

GERTRUDE CHANDLER WARNER discovered when she was teaching that many readers who like an exciting story could find no books that were both easy and fun to read. She decided to try to meet this need, and her first book, *The Boxcar Children*, quickly proved she had succeeded.

Miss Warner drew on her own experiences to write the mystery. As a child she spent hours watching trains go by on the tracks opposite her family home. She often dreamed about what it would be like to set up housekeeping in a caboose or freight car — the situation the Alden children find themselves in.

When Miss Warner received requests for more adventures involving Henry, Jessie, Violet, and Benny Alden, she began additional stories. In each, she chose a special setting and introduced unusual or eccentric characters who liked the unpredictable.

While the mystery element is central to each of Miss Warner's books, she never thought of them as strictly juvenile mysteries. She liked to stress the Aldens' independence and resourcefulness and their solid New England devotion to using up and making do. The Aldens go about most of their adventures with as little adult supervision as possible — something else that delights young readers.

Miss Warner lived in Putnam, Connecticut, until her death in 1979. During her lifetime, she received hundreds of letters from girls and boys telling her how much they liked her books.

Take Me Out to the Ball Game!

The Aldens are on their way to Pikesville, a small town along the Hudson River. Grandfather has a job to do there, but what will Henry, Jessie, Violet, and Benny find to do in this dreary little town? No need to worry — they stumble upon a ballpark and a mystery or two while they're there.

Now you can solve some puzzling mysteries, too. Just grab your pencils and get started on the puzzles and games on the next few pages. You can check your answers at the back of the book. Good luck, and batter up. . . .

Batter Up!

When Henry, Jessie, Violet, and Benny went into the Eagles' clubhouse, they discovered a corked bat. The Eagles were cheating! There are ten bats in this picture, but only one is the corked bat. Can you guess which one it is? It is different from the rest.

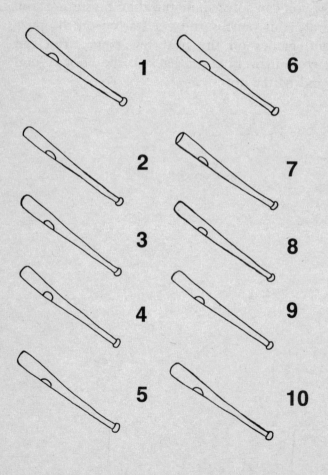

Popcorn! Peanuts!

Benny thinks that what the ballpark really needs is a refreshment stand. Hidden in the ball field below are some things that could be sold at a refreshment stand. Circle all the items you find.

Hudson River Cruise

The Aldens might have thought that Pikesville was dreary, but there are lots of places along the Hudson River that are interesting and beautiful. Can you help them find those places in this word search? Look at the sights marked on the map of the Hudson River area. Then circle all the words you find. The words go up, down, sideways, backward, and diagonally.

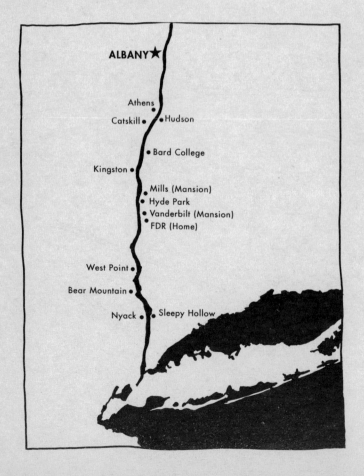

ALBANY ★

Athens
Catskill ● ● Hudson

● Bard College

Kingston ●

Mills (Mansion)
Hyde Park
Vanderbilt (Mansion)
FDR (Home)

West Point ●

Bear Mountain ●

Nyack ● ● Sleepy Hollow

```
C  O  N  I  A  T  N  U  O  M  R  A  E  B  E  W
H  L  C  D  K  D  E  R  A  A  A  E  S  G  T  O  E
T  Y  V  A  E  N  P  R  N  Y  L  P  E  L  E  S
K  I  N  G  S  T  O  N  P  L  E  R  L  L  W  T
C  V  A  N  D  E  R  B  I  L  T  O  L  I  K  P
A  B  I  I  R  K  C  M  D  L  H  N  O  K  A  O
Y  L  T  R  A  F  B  L  S  Y  K  G  C  S  P  I
N  V  D  P  E  B  I  T  P  O  R  C  D  T  L  N
B  A  N  S  F  S  N  E  H  T  A  O  R  A  L  T
A  E  R  D  O  R  E  L  K  E  P  L  A  C  S  K
R  D  R  L  C  L  O  N  L  I  E  P  B  A  T  I
E  G  N  O  S  D  U  H  N  G  D  W  E  S  P  T
L  L  O  C  O  G  O  E  S  T  Y  N  A  B  L  A
H  C  O  K  L  C  L  W  E  Y  H  O  W  E  S  P
```

Home Run King

Herman Soper was nicknamed Home Run Herman because he hit lots and lots of balls into the fence at the ballpark. Now you can make lots and lots of smaller words from the words HOME RUN HER-MAN. Jessie made thirty-one three-, four-, and five-letter words. See if you can break her record!

HOME RUN HERMAN

_____   _____
_____   _____
_____   _____
_____   _____
_____   _____
_____   _____
_____   _____
_____   _____
_____   _____
_____   _____
_____   _____
_____   _____
_____   _____
_____   _____
_____   _____

An A-Mazing Find!

Oh, no! The Percys are in the factory searching for the letter that will clear Home Run Herman's name. And they want to destroy it! Can you help Henry, Jessie, Violet, and Benny find that letter first?

Game Day

It's the day of the big baseball game! Color in this scene any way you want. Try to remember everything you see. Then turn the page and circle the correct answers on the memory test.

Test your memory by answering these questions:

The man with the whistle around his neck is:
a) watching the game from the bleachers
   b) walking into the clubhouse   c) jumping up
   off the bench   d) leaving the ballpark

What is the girl who's waving a flag holding in
her other hand?
a) a hot dog   b) a soda   c) a baseball cap
   d) popcorn

The pitcher is:
a) winding up   b) throwing a pitch   c) throwing
   the ball to second base   d) looking at first
   base

Who is walking out of the clubhouse?
a) a batboy   b) a coach   c) an umpire   d) the
   waterboy

What is written on one of the posters hanging on
the fence?
a) Catskill Eagles   b) Hudson Half Moons
   c) Hat Factory   d) Pikesville

How many kids are sitting in the dugout?
a) twelve   b) ten   c) nine   d) fifteen

A boy sitting in the grandstand is:
a) drinking soda   b) falling asleep   c) spilling
his popcorn   d) waving a flag

Tangled Laces

Oh, no! It's time for the big game, but the Hudson Half Moons can't get to the field because their sneaker laces are all tangled up! Can you help untangle the laces so the team can get out onto the field? Follow the sneakers' laces and match each numbered sneaker with a letter.

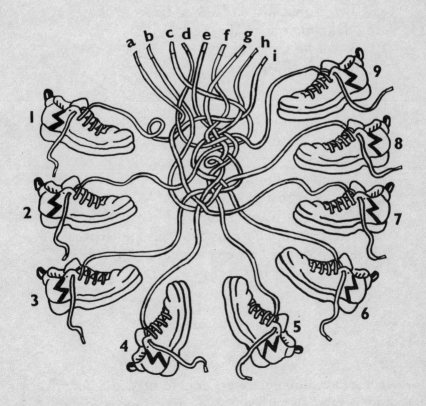

Play Ball!

The Boxcar Children learned a lot about baseball while solving this mystery. Now you can see how much *you* know about baseball by answering the clues and filling in the puzzle. You can use the word list for help.

Across
2. A ball hit high into the air
3. Ball catcher
5. Two games played back-to-back
6. "Take me out to the _____."
10. A ball hit over the fence
11. A swing and a miss

Down
1. The number of innings in a regulation baseball game
2. You need _____ balls for a walk.
4. A four-run home run
5. Two outs made on one play
6. Where the team stays
7. The person who calls the balls and strikes
9. The position between second and third bases

Word List
ball game, doubleheader, double play, dugout, fly, four, grand slam, home run, mitt, nine, shortstop, strike, umpire

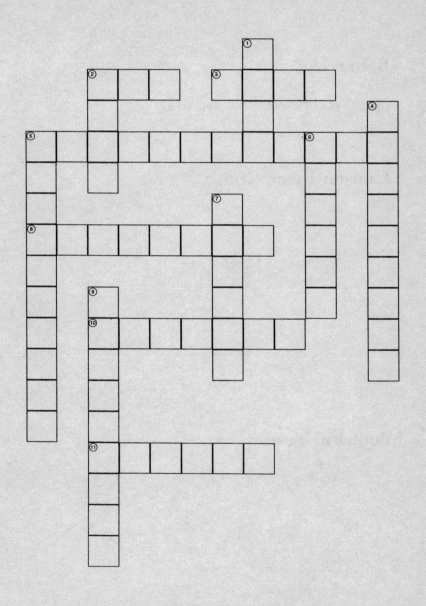

Answers:

Batter Up!

Bat #7 is different from the rest.

Hudson River Cruise

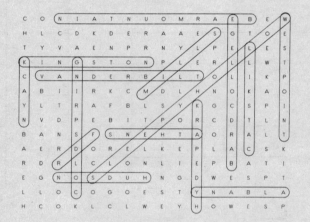

Popcorn! Peanuts!

Home Run King

Possible answers: are, arm, ear, era, ham, her, hum, man, oar, one, ore, ran, run, earn, hare, harm, hear, here, home, mare, mean, more, name, near, none, rear, roam, roar, human, humor, rumor

An A-Mazing Find!

Game Day

c, b, d, a, c, a, c

Tangled Laces

1 goes to i   4 goes to g   7 goes to a
2 goes to c   5 goes to e   8 goes to b
3 goes to f   6 goes to h   9 goes to d

Play Ball!

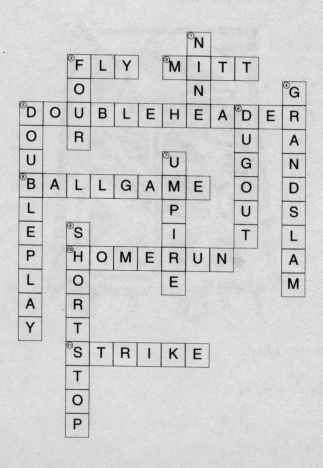